Funny B...

Self-C...

Stella ... Almost

by Wiley Blevins • illustrated by John Nez

RED
CHAIR
• PRESS •

Please visit our website at **www.redchairpress.com**.
Find a free catalog of all our high-quality products for young readers.

Publisher's Cataloging-In-Publication Data
(Prepared by The Donohue Group, Inc.)

Blevins, Wiley.
    Stella ... almost : self-confidence / by Wiley Blevins ; illustrated by John Nez.
-- [First edition].

    pages : illustrations ; cm. -- (Funny bone readers. Dealing with bullies)

    Summary: Stella could do anything she put her mind to ... almost. But when girls
in her class tease her and tell her she's not good at doing the things she likes, Stella
puts away her paper and dance shoes until Grandpa convinces Stella to stop listening
to others and listen to her heart. Includes glossary, as well as questions to self-check
comprehension.
    Interest age level: 004-008.
    Edition statement supplied by publisher.
    Issued also as an ebook.
    ISBN: 978-1-63440-006-0 (library hardcover)
    ISBN: 978-1-63440-007-7 (paperback)

    1. Girls--Juvenile fiction. 2. Bullying--Juvenile fiction. 3. Self-confidence in children-
-Juvenile fiction. 4. Self-doubt--Juvenile fiction. 5. Foxes--Juvenile fiction. 6. Girls-
-Fiction. 7. Bullying--Fiction. 8. Self-confidence--Fiction. 9. Self-doubt--Fiction. 10.
Foxes--Fiction. I. Nez, John A. II. Title.

PZ7.B618652 St 2015
[E]   2014958272

This series first published by:
Red Chair Press LLC   PO Box 333   South Egremont, MA 01258-0333

Printed in the United States of America

042015 1P WRZF15

Stella could do anything.
Almost.

Stella liked to write.

She could write short stories.
She could write long emails.
She could write poems for her fish.

"Your *a's* and *b's* are too crooked,"
said a girl at school. "Mine are better."

So Stella stopped writing.

Stella liked to dance.

She could do jazz.   She could tap.

She could wiggle, shake, and leap.

"Your toes need to be more
pointed," said a girl in her class.
"You aren't very good."

So Stella stopped dancing.

Stella liked to blow bubbles.

She could blow big bubbles.
She could blow little bubbles.
She could blow bubbles shaped
like squares.

"Only babies blow bubbles," said a
kid in the park. "Are you a baby?"

So Stella stopped blowing bubbles.

Then one day Stella's grandpa
came to visit.
"Do you want to write to Grandma?"
he asked.

"I don't write anymore," said Stella. "Someone said my letters are too crooked."

"Then do you want to dance?"
asked Grandpa.
"I don't dance anymore," said Stella.
"Someone said I'm not very good."

"What about blowing bubbles?"
asked Grandpa.
Stella shook her head.

"Well, I think there is one more thing you should stop doing," said Grandpa.
"What?" asked Stella.
"Stop listening to what others say. Listen to your heart."

So Stella grabbed her pencil.
"My letters will get better," she said.

Then she put on her dance shoes.
"Dancing is so much fun," she giggled.

Finally, she handed Grandpa a bubble wand. And together they filled the entire room. Stella once again could do anything . . . almost!

Big Questions: How do you think Stella felt when someone told her she couldn't dance well? Should Stella have listened to what others said to her?

Big Words:

crooked: bent or twisted out of shape, not perfect